Roonerspisms

Dr. Gary Pillow

To Miss Miller,
my wonderful
second grade
teacher,
♡ gary

To order additional copies of this book, contact:
Xlibris
844-714-8691
www.Xlibris.com
Orders@Xlibris.com

ISBN: Softcover   978-1-6698-1344-6
         Hardcover   978-1-6698-1343-9
         EBook   978-1-6698-1345-3

Library of Congress Control Number: 2022903551

Print information available on the last page

Rev. date: 02/23/2022

I want to dedicate this book to my beautiful wife and lifelong friend, Denise and also to those who call me Dad:

Jonathan, Nicholas, Hannah, Leah and Daniel and to those who call me G'Paw:

Lucas, Lucy, Susannah, Elyza, Corbin, Nolan, Chezley, Alison & Marley

Acknowledgement: Thank you for your artistic
input Carol Marlowe Nelms!

INTRODUCTION

Phoneme manipulation skills are very important in the development of early reading. The manipulation of phonemes is "playing around" with sounds in words to make new words. This includes inserting, deleting, and/or substituting sounds within words. Phoneme manipulation is one area of phonological awareness. Phonological awareness is the awareness of sound structure of words, and is a very reliable predictor of future reading ability. Therefore, these skills are necessary for the development of good reading and spelling in early readers.

Spoonerisms are made by switching the first sounds of two words to make two new words. I have switched the sounds within Spoonerism, although only one word, to create the title of this book. ROONERSPISMS is one way to show young children how changing the first sounds in words changes their meaning. I hope you will enjoy the whimsical pictures and learn how much fun it can be to play with words!

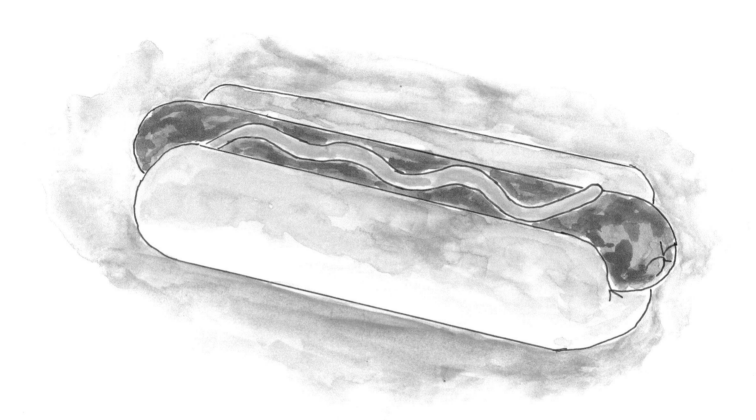

Hot Dog

Dot Hog

Trail Snacks

Snail Tracks

Mend the Sail

Send the Mail

Save the Whale

Wave the Sail

Bunny Hair

Honey Bear

Toe Nail

No Tail

Butterfly

Flutter By

Taking a Shower

Shaking a Tower

White Lizard

Light Wizard

Fireplace

Plier Face

Bedroom

Red Boom

Tugboat

Bug Tote

My House

Hi, Mouse!

Blushing Crow

Crushing Blow

Doing the Chores

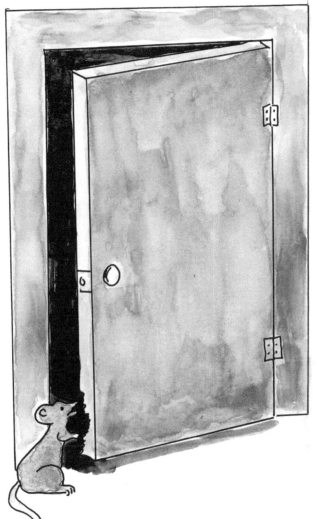

Chewing the Doors

Eyeball

Bye-all

CPSIA information can be obtained
at www.ICGtesting.com
Printed in the USA
BVHW022128020322
630548BV00011B/44